Hooray
for
Anna
Hibiscus!

Hooray for ANNA HIBISCUS!

by Atinuke

Illustrated by Lauren Tobia

Kane Miller
A DIVISION OF EDC PUBLISHING

First American Edition 2010
Kane Miller, A Division of EDC Publishing

First published in 2007 by Walker Books Ltd., London (England)
Text © 2007 Atinuke
Illustrations © 2007 Lauren Tobia

Library of Congress Control Number: 2009943492

Printed and bound in the United States of America
9 10 11 12 13 14 15 16 17 18
ISBN: 978-1-61067-784-4

To my sisters,
OE and TJ, the original
Double and Trouble
A.

To all the babies,
Hannah, Max, Billy, Finn,
Niamh and Ciara
L.T.

"Anna 'biscus! Sing!"

Anna Hibiscus lives in Africa. Amazing Africa. She lives with her mother and her father; her grandmother and her grandfather; her aunties and her uncles; her cousins, little, medium and big; and her twin baby brothers, Double and Trouble. They all live together in a big white house.

7

Anna Hibiscus stays at home all day long with the little cousins. Little cousins do not go to school. They help their mothers and aunties with the work of the big white house, and they play in the beautiful, flower-filled garden.

Anna Hibiscus loves helping her mother
and her aunties wash clothes. She loves
feeding the chickens and climbing the
mango trees to pick the sweet fruit. But
especially and particularly, Anna Hibiscus
loves singing. She loves singing to her
brothers, Double and Trouble, all day long.

Double and Trouble are still babies. They are only just now saying something. They have three new words that Anna Hibiscus is always listening out for.

Trouble's two words are "Anna 'biscus!"

And Double's word is "Sing!"

And if ever they are confused, if ever they are bored or tired, Double and Trouble shout:

"Anna 'biscus!"

"Sing!"

And Anna comes running from wherever she is to sing to her brothers. Because Anna Hibiscus loves her brothers, and Anna Hibiscus loves to sing.

This Christmas, for the very first time,
Anna Hibiscus will see snow – in Canada!
So she sings about snow:

"Snow, you are wonderful!
I will see and tell you so!
Snow, you are so cold-o!
I will feel and say you so!
Snow, you are so sweet-o!
I will taste and tell you so!"

All day long while Anna is singing and playing at home, her father and the uncles and some of the aunties are working hard in their offices and businesses and churches to make Africa a Better Place.

One day Anna Hibiscus's father came home from work. "I want to talk to you, Anna Hibiscus," he said. "I need to explain something important. You are still small, but you are growing bigger every day. You are growing up! And growing-up children have work to do. Work to make Africa – and the whole entire world – a Better Place."

"What work, Papa?" Anna Hibiscus asked.

"It is this," Anna Hibiscus's father said. "Now you are growing up, you must go to school."

Anna Hibiscus was sad. She did not want to go to school where she knew nobody and nobody knew her (except for a few cousins). She did not want to leave the big white house.

But the next school day, her mother
came to call her, and Anna Hibiscus was
very brave. She got up early and put on
a clean school uniform that used to belong
to her big cousin Clarity and said goodbye
to Grandmother and Grandfather and her
mother and her father and the aunties and
the uncles and the little cousins and the
chickens and the goats and the mango trees
and the big white house and the beautiful
garden and Double Trouble, and squeezed
into the car with all the other growing-up
cousins and went to school.

All morning while she was at school, Anna Hibiscus missed everybody and everything in the big white house and the beautiful, wide compound. But most especially and enormously, she missed Double Trouble. She was so far away she could not hear them say, "Anna 'biscus! Sing!" So every outside break time, Anna Hibiscus sang as loudly as she could in the direction of the big white house, just in case they could hear her.

One night when Anna Hibiscus's mother and father and aunties and uncles came back from their work, they were full of talk. They called all the cousins and the stay-at-home aunties and Grandmother and Grandfather and told everybody that for the very first time, the president of a country outside of Africa was coming to visit their own country.

"Ours is only one of many countries in Africa," began Uncle Tunde.

"We must show this president how wonderful our country is," Auntie Joly said.

"And how important things are here," Anna's father added.

"But most important of all," Grandfather said gently, "this president will be our guest. We must make sure she is comfortable and at ease."

"Then, when she goes away," Grandmother said, "she will have only kind-hearted feelings towards our country and our people."

Everybody agreed.

At school the next day, everybody was talking about the same thing.

Anna Hibiscus's teacher announced, "There will be a big welcoming ceremony in the National Stadium for the visiting president. Our school has been asked to participate. We must send a good speaker, a good dancer and a good singer."

She chose a good speaker and a good dancer, and then she said, "Hands up who can sing."

Many children's hands went up. They all wanted to sing in the National Stadium for the important president. Anna Hibiscus sat on her hands. She did not want to sing in

front of the president. What if she did not like Anna's song? Then she would go away with no good feelings for Anna's country. And it would all be the fault of Anna and her useless song.

The teacher looked at the children. She had never heard them sing. She did not know who to pick.

Then Anna's cousin Angel said, "Anna Hibiscus can sing!"

"Yes! Yes!" everybody shouted. "It is true! It is true! Anna Hibiscus is singing all the time."

The teacher made Anna Hibiscus stand up. "Sing, Anna," she said.

Anna Hibiscus stood up. She did not
know what to sing.

"Sing 'Snow,'" Angel whispered.

So Anna Hibiscus sang her favorite song
about snow.

"It is true," said the teacher, when Anna
had finished. "Anna Hibiscus, you can sing!
We will send you!"

Back at the big white house, Chocolate and Angel told everybody, "Anna Hibiscus is going to sing for the visiting president!"

"What is this?" everybody asked Anna.

"It is true," Anna Hibiscus said. "My school is going to send me to sing for the president."

"At the National Stadium!" said Chocolate.

"She is going to sing all on her own!" said Angel.

Anna Hibiscus felt very sorry for herself. Double and Trouble looked at her worried face. They felt worried too. "Anna 'biscus! Sing! Anna 'biscus! Sing!" they shouted.

So Anna Hibiscus sang for them until she felt much better.

And now Anna did not mind going to school so much. She did not do mathematics and spelling anymore. She only sang and sang and sang her new president song!

And in the afternoon when she got home, Double Trouble shouted, "Anna 'biscus! Anna 'biscus! Sing! Sing!"

And Anna Hibiscus sang her new president song.

20

And at night when Double and Trouble went to bed, Anna Hibiscus sang it to them again. It was their new favorite song!

"Welcome to our beautiful country,
Welcome to our wonderful land.
Welcome to the sun shining brightly,
Welcome to our cool evening rain..."

Morning, noon and night, Anna Hibiscus sang this song. She did not tire of singing it. It was *her* new favorite song too.

Anna Hibiscus was happy singing
at school and at home. But one day she
went to practice at the National Stadium,
and she was not happy anymore. The stage
was as big as a soccer field. There were
thousands of seats in front and all around.
Anna felt very small on that stage. She felt
as small as an ant. An ant standing alone
under World Cup lights.

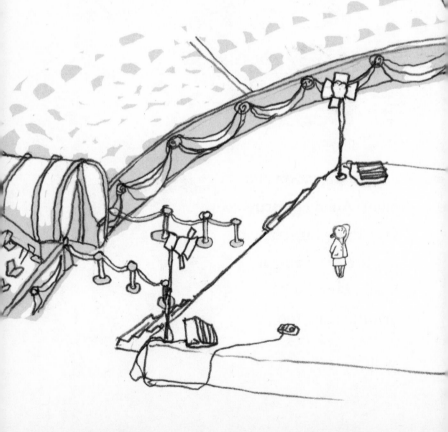

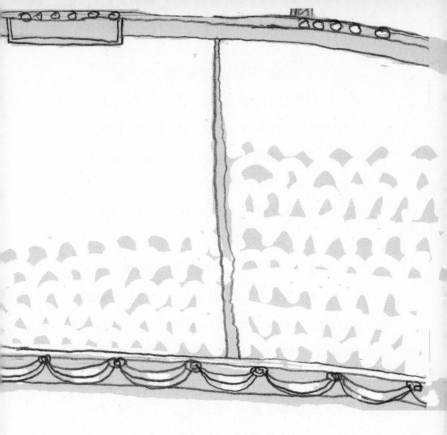

"Don't worry," said Chocolate, when
Anna came home, "we will be there. It will
be us sitting there. Don't be afraid."

"Don't worry," said Angel. "You know you
can sing. We all know you can sing."

"Sing! Sing!" said Double happily, and
Trouble clapped his hands.

On the night the president arrived, everybody in Anna Hibiscus's family was there waiting at the National Stadium. Her mother and her father and all of their friends. Her grandmother and her grandfather and all of their friends. Her aunties and her uncles and all of their friends. Her cousins, little, medium and big, and all of their friends! Even Double and Trouble were there. They were noisy babies who were meant to be left at home, but they cried so much at being left behind that Anna's mother and father took pity on them and brought them along too.

Up on the stage many adults and children made long speeches of welcome. Traditional dances were performed by many schools. The big national choir sang welcome songs.

Then it was the turn of Anna Hibiscus.

Anna stood alone on the stage. On a stage big enough for a soccer game,

Anna stood alone. A sea of faces rose in front of her, but the lights shone in her eyes, and she could not see one face she knew. There was nobody standing beside her or behind her. Nobody to hold her hand or sing with her. There were only all those people looking at her; and one of those people, Anna knew, was a president from a strange and faraway country.

Anna forgot her song.

The audience was silent. Everybody was waiting for the small girl on stage to speak or sing or dance or do something. The visiting president looked at her watch.

Anna Hibiscus did nothing. She did not know her song anymore. Her throat was a dry riverbed. Her bones had turned to stone. She could not move. Not even to run off the stage.

Anna Hibiscus's mother and father, grandmother and grandfather, aunties and uncles, cousins and friends, all looked at one another. They held their breath and waited.

And waited.

Double was bored. He climbed up
on his chair. Trouble was bored. He too
stood up on his chair. Anna's mother and
the aunties struggled to make them sit
down. Double and Trouble could see Anna
Hibiscus standing there on the stage alone.
Double and Trouble were confused. They
were bored. They were tired. There was
only one thing to do.

"Anna 'biscus!" Trouble shouted.

"Sing!" shouted Double.

Alone on the stage, Anna Hibiscus heard the brothers she loved shout. She looked up, and there they were! Out in the audience, above everybody else!

Suddenly Anna Hibiscus was not alone. Her bones came alive. Her throat was no longer dry. She remembered her song! It ran like a river! Anna opened her mouth and sang!

"Welcome to our beautiful country,
Welcome to our wonderful land.
Welcome to the sun shining brightly,
Welcome to our cool evening rain.
Welcome to our flowers always
blooming,
Welcome to our trees always green.
Welcome to our rivers of fishes,
Welcome to our farms growing food.
Welcome to our deep dark rain forest,
Welcome to our industries' sound.
Welcome to our schools full of
children,
Welcome to our cities and towns.
Welcome to our beautiful country,
Welcome to our sweet motherland!"

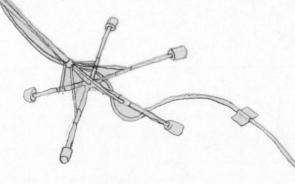

The audience clapped and clapped and clapped. The foreign president stood up on her feet and clapped. Anna's family and friends stood up on their feet and clapped. Everybody stood up and clapped.

"Hooray!" shouted Grandfather.

"Hooray!" shouted Grandmother.

"Hooray!" shouted her mother and father and aunties and uncles and cousins and friends and everybody else.

"Hooray! Anna 'biscus!" shouted Trouble.

"Anna 'biscus! Hooray!" shouted Double.

They were clapping the longest and shouting the loudest.

"Hooray! Hooray! Hooray!"

It was their new word.

Your Hair, Anna Hibiscus!

Anna Hibiscus lives with her whole
entire family in Africa. Wonderful Africa.
Amazing Africa. Africa, where girls have
beautiful hair. Short or long, the hair of an
African girl is thicker and shinier and curlier
than any other hair in the whole world.

Everybody in Anna's family must look after their hair. They must oil it so that it shines and sparkles in the sunlight. They must comb it well-well. Anna's grandfather, father, uncles and boy cousins have short-short hair.

Oil, comb, and the palaver is over. Not so for Anna Hibiscus and her girl cousins with their long-long hair. Not so for her aunties. For them the headache has only just begun.

Grandmother and Grandfather say it is best to observe the traditional African ways, and the whole family agrees.

Traditional African women and girls braid and weave their hair. That is how such thick and curly hair stays shiny and beautiful and neat, with no chemicals whatsoever.

But Anna Hibiscus knows that braiding and weaving mean hours and hours of hair-pulling and head-squeezing and scalp-yanking. Anna Hibiscus hates her hair. It is too thick; it is too curly. Never mind that it is beautiful and shiny. Anna Hibiscus *hates* it.

And one day Anna Hibiscus decides she cannot stand looking after it anymore.

37

It was one Friday evening. Anna Hibiscus was sitting on the floor while her cousin Joy loosened all her tiny-tiny braids. Anna was uncomfortable; Anna was bored; Anna was cross. Every Friday evening was the same. Pull! Tug! Yank! The braids that had been holding her thick hair tight and neat all week had to be loosened, ready to be weaved tight and neat again the next day.

All around the room, Grandmother was helping aunties, aunties were helping big girl cousins, and big girl cousins were helping little girl cousins to loosen all the tiny-tiny tight-tight braids on each others' heads.

Anna's head was pulled first one way and then the other. She was getting crosser and more uncomfortable, but she did not dare complain.

"Do you see anybody else complaining?" her aunties would ask.

Anna Hibiscus did not. Nobody else complained. Even the smallest of small girl cousins did not complain. They all tried to be as brave as their mothers. But the aunties' heads must be so hard by now, Anna thought. After centuries of pulling and tugging and yanking, their heads must be as hard as concrete.

Auntie Joly combed Anna Hibiscus's loosened hair. How any knots could have entered it when it had been weaved so tightly for the whole one week, Anna

Hibiscus would never know. But knots were always there. The comb put them there on purpose.

Now it was Anna's turn to have her hair washed. Her mother's fingers were soft and gentle, rubbing her sore scalp.

Anna's hair was dried and then oiled and then combed again. Already there were more knots!

This thin comb would tangle anybody's hair, Anna Hibiscus thought crossly.

At last one of the big cousins put Anna's hair into thick, easy braids to keep it neat until tomorrow.

Anna Hibiscus was tired of the pulling and the tugging and the yanking; and tomorrow, she knew, would be worse. Suddenly Anna Hibiscus made a decision.

Tomorrow the Saturday weaving aunties would come. Those Saturday weaving aunties who were not her aunties; who were nobodies' aunties that she knew; who she had to call auntie just to be polite. Tomorrow she would have to sit on the floor between the knees of one of those aunties. And those knees, fat or thin, those knees would grip her head firmly in place. Then the fingers of the Saturday weaving auntie would pull and pull and pull tiny fingerfuls of Anna Hibiscus's hair until Anna was surprised that her hair was not being pulled right out and falling on the ground.

And every Saturday Anna shouted and shouted because she could not help shouting

when someone was pulling out fingerfuls
of her hair. And everybody would laugh
and say, "Anna Hibiscus, you must have
a head as soft as a baby!"

Anna was furious just thinking about it.

The next morning, Grandmother and all
the aunties and the girl cousins were up
early waiting for the Saturday weaving
aunties to come and weave their hair. But
Anna Hibiscus was up even earlier. Before
the first cock crow, she peeped out of her
bedroom door, looking right, looking left.
Then she tiptoed down the corridor.

Oh no!
Here was
Grandmother!
Anna Hibiscus
flattened herself
against the wall.
Grandmother went
the other way.

Anna Hibiscus
continued to
tiptoe down
the hall.
Oh no!
Here was
Uncle Tunde!

She peeped down
the stairs. Nobody
there. Nobody except…
Oh no! Anna Hibiscus
shot back into
the corridor.
She could not
go down those
stairs without her
mother seeing her.

Anna Hibiscus tiptoed to another set of
stairs that led straight outside. She started
to go down... Oh no! Here was Uncle
Bizi Sunday! Anna Hibiscus was stuck!
The cockerel from next door flew over the
wall looking for hens and trouble. Oh no!
Now the squawking and the crowing
and the shouting would wake
everybody up!

Quick, Anna Hibiscus ran down the stairs, around the corner of the house and jumped into the back of an empty car. She ran all that way and – lucky for her – nobody saw her. Not Grandmother, not Mother, not Uncle Tunde, not Uncle Bizi Sunday, not the cockerel. Only the hens saw her, and they wouldn't tell.

Now everybody was up. Big cousins rushed to breakfast untying their braids. Little cousins were caught to have their hair loosened. Aunties chose designs and held little cousins in place and exchanged news with the Saturday weaving aunties. Everybody was so loud and so busy that nobody noticed – Anna Hibiscus was not there!

It was only just before they left that one of the Saturday weaving aunties asked, "Where dey de small one who like to shout?"

Grandmother, aunties and cousins looked around for Anna Hibiscus.

"It's Anna's turn to oil the little ones' hair!" complained Chocolate.

"Anna! Where have you gone?"

Suddenly everybody was asking, "Where is Anna? Where is Anna? Where has Anna Hibiscus gone?"

The big boy cousins were told to look for her high up in the fruit trees.

Chocolate and
Angel were sent to
the girls' bedrooms
to search.

Uncle Tunde
opened cupboards
and took lids off pots.
Anna's mother
texted Anna's father,
who had gone to buy
newspapers. But he did
not know where Anna
was. Anna Hibiscus
was searched for high
and low. Above and
below. Before and
behind. Inside and out.
And she was not found.

She was not found until one hour later,
when the Saturday weaving aunties had gone.

"Anna Hibiscus, what happened to you?" everybody asked.

"Ah-ah, Anna Hibiscus. We were worrying about you!" said Grandmother.

"I was asleep," said Anna. Which was true. But she did not say *where*.

"Anna Hibiscus, the Saturday weaving aunties, dey have all gone!" said Angel.

"Good!" said Anna Hibiscus.

Anna's grandmother, her mother and the aunties looked at one another.

"But what about your hair?" asked Chocolate, worried.

"I don't care."

The aunties opened their mouths wide-wide.

"Leave her," said Grandmother. "She will learn."

I will, thought Anna happily. I will learn how to do my hair properly without all that pulling and tugging and yanking.

Anna Hibiscus was very proud of herself.
She had made a decision and carried it out.

That night, before eating, Anna loosened
her thick braids and put her hair into two
neat pompoms. She tied the pompoms with
ribbons. It took about two minutes, and Anna
Hibiscus felt very pretty, and very, very happy.

At bedtime, Anna Hibiscus refused to take
out the pompoms and put the thick braids
back in.

"Leave her," said Grandmother again.

The next morning, Anna Hibiscus's
pompoms were squashed and full of knots.

Anna Hibiscus went to her mother and
father's room. She put her father's softening
oil on her hair and tried to brush out the knots
with her mother's soft brush. The brush stuck
fast. Anna had to pull the brush to get it out
of her hair. She had to pull it hard. "Ow!"
Anna shaped the knotty pompoms with
her fingers and went downstairs.

Grandfather sent her back upstairs.

"You can't go to church like that," he said.
Anna found a pretty head tie
to cover her squashed and
knotty pompoms.

"Tomorrow is
school," said Cousin
Clarity. "You can't go
to school with your
hair in a head tie.
It's not allowed."

On Monday morning, Anna Hibiscus took out the squashed and knotty pompoms and tried to smooth her hair with her hands before she went downstairs. Little cousins looked at her sticking-up-and-out hair with big eyes. Big cousins looked with worried eyes. Anna's mother, aunties and uncles and grandmother looked away.

Nobody offered to help Anna Hibiscus, and Anna Hibiscus did not ask for anybody's help. No more pulling and tugging and yanking from them. No, thank you!

At school the other children laughed at Anna Hibiscus's hair, but Anna Hibiscus pretended not to care.

Anna's hair grew worse and worse. Every night more and more knots jumped into her hair, and every morning it was more and more impossible to comb.

On Tuesday morning Anna Hibiscus spent a long time alone with her father's comb. But the knots would not budge. She cried as she tried to comb out the knots and tangles. She cried as she pulled and tugged and yanked her own hair. She cried when the children at school teased her.

On Wednesday morning she took the comb to her mother.

"Oh, Anna!" her mother sighed.

Anna's mother tried to help, but Anna's mother's hair was straight; she did not know a lot about curly hair. The little girl cousins tried to help: they pulled and tugged and yanked. But it was no use. Anna Hibiscus's hair was one big knot.

On Thursday morning the teacher said, "Anna Hibiscus, go home and come back when you do not look so disgraceful."

Anna Hibiscus did not tell anybody what the teacher said. But on Friday morning she hid.

After the other cousins had gone to school, Grandmother came to find Anna. Anna's hair was still thicker and curlier than any hair anywhere in the world, but it was no longer shiny and beautiful. It was rough and dry and sticking up in every place.

"Come with me, Anna Hibiscus," said Grandmother. "Let me help you now."

Grandmother rubbed thick grease in Anna's hair to soften it. She wet it to loosen the knots. She spent a long time softly, softly loosening the knots with her gentle fingers. Then she had to pull and tug and yank with the comb, but Anna did not complain. She was grateful to Grandmother for helping her. Some of the knots were so tight that Grandmother had to cut them out with scissors. Tears rolled down Anna's face as she saw her beautiful hair fall to the ground. But she did not shout.

"Anna Hibiscus, your hair! It is short now!" cried the other girl cousins when they saw her.

But Anna Hibiscus did not care. Her problems were over. Grandmother had loosened them and cut them all out.

Anna Hibiscus was happy. Tomorrow
the Saturday weaving aunties would come.
They would weave her hair into short but
beautiful braids. Braids that would stay on
her head for one whole week, not causing
any trouble, not requiring any combing,
pulling, tugging or yanking! No more teasing
or worrying or hiding. Anna Hibiscus would
be able to hold her head high all week!

Saturday came and, for the first time
ever, Anna Hibiscus did not shout even
one shout.

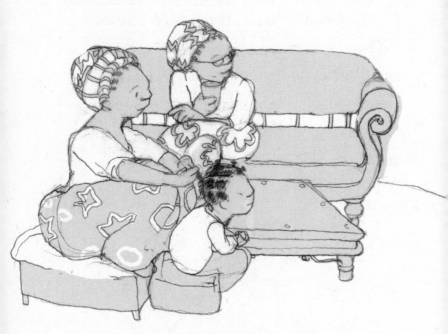

No, while her hair was pulled and
tugged and yanked in tiny fingerfuls,
Anna Hibiscus smiled.

Anna Hibiscus and the New Generator

Anna Hibiscus lives in Africa. Amazing Africa. She lives with her whole family in a big white house in a beautiful garden in the middle of a big compound.

Like every other family in Africa, the evening is a busy time for Anna's family. Clothes must be washed and rinsed and hung up to dry. Food must be prepared while it is still light.

"Change your clothes!" shouts Auntie Joly at the cousins returning from school.

"Come and pound yam!" calls Anna's mother when she gets home from work.

Anna Hibiscus runs to loose Double from her mother's back. She is too small to pound yam, but she is big enough to look after Double, and she is big enough to wash her school clothes ready for the next day.

Food is cooked and eaten and cleared away. It is now dark outside. But in the lit-up house, there is still a lot going on.

The bright and shining house is full of noise. The air conditioners are loud, and the television is even louder. Small cousins are crying and whining because they are tired and do not want to go to bed. Double and Trouble whine the loudest of all.

Even outside on the veranda the radio is talking and singing above the voices of the uncles. Only Grandmother and Grandfather are still and quiet, dozing in a corner. Soon

Double and Trouble will crawl onto their soft laps and fall asleep.

One night Anna Hibiscus and her cousins were watching television; aunties were sewing on noisy machines; big cousins were homeworking under bright lights; uncles were arguing with the radio.

Suddenly the lights went out! The radio and television were quenched. The air conditioners and sewing machines fell silent.

Electricity was gone!

This is quite normal in Africa. If electricity is there, it is there. If it is gone, it is gone. No point asking questions. That is how it is in Africa. Everything is unpredictable. You can count on it.

Now it was **DARK**. Now it was **QUIET**. Anna Hibiscus could see nothing. But she could hear her heart pounding in her chest. She could hear the frogs croak and the mosquitoes whine. She could hear the slap of the lagoon water on the city's dry banks and the roar of the cars in the dark streets. It was dark. It was quiet. It was wonderful!

For a moment, nobody moved, not an inch, not uncles or aunties or cousins. Nobody moved except for Grandmother and Grandfather. They sat bolt upright. Awake! Double and Trouble shuffled on their laps. Then suddenly aunties and uncles and big cousins were calling and searching for matches and candles and flashlights. Double and Trouble rubbed their eyes.

Anna Hibiscus jumped up and down and yelled, "Hooray! Hooray!"

Little cousins ran shouting. Chocolate and Angel played hide-and-seek in the candlelight and dark. Double and Trouble looked around with big, wide eyes at the deep shadows and the dancing yellow candles and the beams of white flashlight. Grandfather made a cool breeze with his fan. It was wonderful.

The big cousins came downstairs. They had to do their homework at the table by the light of the paraffin lamp. Aunties drifted out to talk with uncles on the veranda. There were jokes and laughing. The uncles teased the aunties with songs, and the aunties laughed and danced and softly clapped their hands. The swish-swish of Grandfather's fan joined in.

Then Grandmother told a story. The homework stopped; the jokes and the dancing and the songs stopped. The whole family gathered to listen to Grandmother. Even Double and Trouble sat quietly. One by one the little cousins fell asleep. When Grandmother's stories stopped they would be carried by flashlight to bed. Through the screens of the open bedroom windows, the songs of the frogs and the lagoon would last throughout the night. Wonderful!

One evening Anna's father and the uncles said, "We have an announcement! We have bought a generator. Now when the electricity fails we will still have light!"

The big cousins shouted happily; the aunties exclaimed loudly; Grandmother and Grandfather looked interested. Anna Hibiscus was excited. What did this mean?

Men came with a truck. A big machine
was unloaded and stationed underneath
Anna Hibiscus's favorite mango tree.
Anna started to look worried.

Two evenings later, the lights went out.
The air conditioners and sewing machines and
radio and television fell silent. It was dark. It
was quiet. It was wonderful. Grandmother and
Grandfather sat up. Double and Trouble stirred.
The frogs croaked; the lagoon sang. The uncles
ran outside to turn on the generator.

A huge engine noise was heard, and the lights
came back on! The rooms were bright and the
television loud again. Cheers and shouts were
heard from every corner of the house.

The cousins continued with their homework
upstairs. They had not even had time
to come down. Aunties who were starting
to joke went back to their television
and sewing machines. Triumphant
uncles congratulated each other
and went back to the radio on the
veranda. Double and Trouble
started to cry. Anna Hibiscus

and the little cousins looked sadly at one
another. There had been no flashlight or
candles. There had been no hide-and-seek.

Anna could see Grandmother and Grandfather in the corner. They looked small and old. Grandmother started to say something, but nobody heard her. The noise of the generator and the televisions and the radio and the air conditioners and the sewing machines was too loud. Grandmother went back to sleep. The story she would have told was gone.

Grandfather had lifted his fan ready to cool himself, but the air conditioners were already back on. Slowly, he lowered it. He looked sadly at Anna Hibiscus and Double and Trouble.

Double and Trouble cried and cried until they were taken upstairs to bed. They were confused; they were upset.

Now, every day, the uncles were out with the new generator. Polishing it and oiling it and tightening it up with tools. Double and Trouble and all the cousins, little, medium and big, watched – but they were not allowed to touch.

The new generator was right underneath Anna Hibiscus's favorite mango tree. Now whenever she came out to climb her tree, it was full of big cousins looking down at the generator. It was crowded with uncles and little cousins admiring the generator.

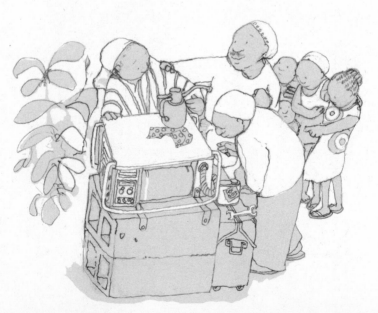

It was busy with friends come to congratulate the uncles. The ground was littered with tools and oil and rags.

Anna Hibiscus sucked her teeth! This is what you do in Africa when you are not at all happy with somebody ... or something. Anna Hibiscus sucked her teeth again. What was that machine doing underneath her tree? What was it doing in her compound at all? It had come and swallowed Grandmother's stories, and the songs of the frogs and the lagoon. It had come and blown out the candlelight and the flashlight and the jokes of the aunties and uncles. It had come and stolen the games little cousins played in the dark. It had filled the wide eyes of babies full of tears.

Anna Hibiscus did not like the generator at-all at-all.

There was somebody else who did not like that generator. Somebody else who knew it was in the way. Pronto, the old he-goat with the long, strong horns. Pronto liked to scratch his back on the very same branch the generator stood beneath. Now the generator was blocking the branch.

One day, at last, the uncles and cousins were busy with something else, their friends had gone home, and the aunties had returned to their work. Anna Hibiscus climbed her tree alone, in peace. But the generator was still there. Pronto was chewing and glaring at it.

Suddenly the generator *twanged*! It *wanged* and it *clanged*! Anna Hibiscus clung to her branch and looked down. The generator was alive!

Pronto stared at the generator. His rival had spoken. Pronto rammed the big machine with his long, strong horns. If ever a younger he-goat were to walk into the compound, Pronto would deal with him just so.

He butted it hard again and again. The generator *clanged* and *twanged* and *shouted*! Anna was frozen on her branch. She did not know what to do!

The old goat was strong, but the generator did not move one inch. Pronto gave up and walked off stiffly. He had not yet succeeded in driving his rival away, but at least he had taught him a lesson.

The generator was silent. A tool came flying out from behind it. The tool was followed first by Trouble and then by Double. Anna Hibiscus's mouth fell open! It had been Double and Trouble *twanging* and *wanging* the generator!

Anna Hibiscus stayed up in the tree for a long time, thinking. She decided to say nothing. She climbed down.

The next time the electricity went off and the uncles came to switch on the generator, it would not start. There was no joking or laughing or dancing that night. The aunties sat sighing at their silent sewing machines. Big cousins stared at each other over their homework. Only the little cousins were happy; only Grandmother and Grandfather were content; only Double and Trouble rubbed their eyes and smiled.

The uncles called a mechanic, but there was nothing he could do. The generator was broken. Kaput. Anna Hibiscus's mother and father, her aunties and uncles and all the big cousins were very sad.

Anna Hibiscus could not stop thinking about Double and Trouble and the generator and Pronto ramming it, and herself up in the tree saying nothing and still saying nothing now! Anna Hibiscus could not stop thinking, but she did not know what to do.

Grandmother and Grandfather noticed. They noticed that when the lights went out, Anna Hibiscus no longer shouted "Hooray!" She no longer laughed and ran and played hide-and-seek.

One day when the house was quiet and empty, they called her.

"What is the matter, Anna Hibiscus?" Grandfather asked.

"Nothing, Grandfather," replied Anna.

"Are you missing the generator?" Grandmother asked gently.

Anna burst into tears.

Grandmother and Grandfather looked
at each other. Anna Hibiscus told them the
whole story. She told them how the generator
had come alive and how Pronto had rammed
it, and how a tool had come flying out from
behind it followed by Double and Trouble.

Grandmother and Grandfather laughed
and laughed. They could not stop. Double
and Trouble crawled over to join in the fun.
They did not know why Grandmother and
Grandfather were laughing, but they wanted
to laugh too.

"Hooray!" shouted
Double happily.

Now Anna started
to laugh. She could not
help herself. Grandmother
and Grandfather, Anna
Hibiscus, and Double
and Trouble laughed
and laughed.

That night, when the whole family was gathered to eat, Grandfather made an announcement.

"Generators," said Grandfather, "are very un-traditional. They are guzzlers of money. They are destroyers of the peace. God has ordained some nights for modern, busy noisiness, and others for more traditional pursuits. God gives us electricity some nights and takes it away other nights. This is a balance between modern and traditional. Our family will spend no more money on disturbing this balance. No more generators in this compound!"

Anna Hibiscus breathed a sigh of relief. Now she need not say anything about Double and Trouble and Pronto and the generator to anybody else. They had probably been acting under Grandfather's orders. Or God's.

That night, in the dark and quiet,
Grandmother's stories were about
an old he-goat, troublesome but wise!

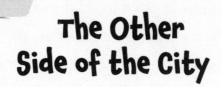

The Other
Side of the City

Anna Hibiscus lives with her mother
and her father; her grandmother and her
grandfather; her aunties and their husbands;
her uncles and their wives; all her many,
many cousins; and her two baby brothers.
They all live together in a big white house
in a large, quiet compound in a huge, busy
city in the middle of a wonderful country
on the amazing continent of Africa.

The city that Anna Hibiscus lives in is full
of roads and lagoons, full of cars and boats, full
of people. Poor people and rich people, all rush
and hurry. Anna's compound is quiet – much
quieter than the busy-busy city outside the
gate with its millions of people and thousands
of roads and hundreds of lagoons.

Anna Hibiscus often looks through
the gate to the lagoon on the other side of
the road. It is crowded with boats coming
and going from the other side of the city.

"Come and play, Anna Hibiscus,"
said Cousin Sweetheart one day.

"Why are you always looking outside?"
asked Cousin Joy.

Anna wanted to go on the ferry across
the lagoon. Anna wanted to see the other
side of the city. That was why she was
always looking and looking.

"What can there be to see?" said Cousin
Wonderful. "It can only be more houses like
this. More people like us."

But still Anna wanted to go. Still Anna
had to see.

Uncle Bizi Sunday often went on one of those lagoon ferry boats. Uncle Bizi Sunday had people he went to see on the other side of the city. Anna Hibiscus decided to ask him, again.

"Stop troubling me!" said Uncle Bizi Sunday.

Auntie Joly also went to the other side of the city. She took clothes sometimes to a home for motherless babies there. Anna decided to ask her.

"Anna Hibiscus," Auntie Joly sighed,
"why do you want to go to the other side
of the city? The people there are poor.
It is not a good place. The other side of the
city has nothing to do with you."

So Anna Hibiscus
asked Uncle Tunde
and her other
uncles.

She asked
Auntie Grace and
her other aunties.

They all said the same
thing. "It is a poor
place. It is not
a good place.
Why does it
concern you?"

Anna asked Grandmother and Grandfather, "Is it bad to be poor? Is it wrong?"

"No," said Grandmother. "It is not bad. It is not wrong. But it is not easy to be very poor."

"It is not easy to look at poverty either," Anna's mother added.

"It is not nice to be very poor, and it is not nice to see, Anna Hibiscus," said her father. "The other side of the city is not for you."

But still Anna Hibiscus wanted to go.

"Let her go," said Grandfather. "Let her see; let her know."

Anna Hibiscus jumped up and down! Hooray! Hooray! She was going on a ferry. She was going to cross the lagoon. She was going to see the other side of the city!

"Thank you, Grandfather! Thank you!" she shouted, and ran to tell Sweetheart and Joy and Wonderful and all the other cousins.

"Let her see and know just how lucky she is," said Grandfather, sighing.

Anna Hibiscus got ready. She oiled her neatly braided hair. She chose her best pink Sunday dress, her favorite hair ribbons and her new Sunday shoes.

"Remove the shoes," said Auntie Joly. "Do you want to spoil them in the boat?"

Anna Hibiscus put her shoes back in the cupboard. She put on her old pink flip-flops. All flip-flops Anna's size were pink. Other sizes were other colors.

Auntie Joly and Uncle Bizi Sunday were going to take Anna on the ferry. Auntie Joly wore one of her old dresses; Uncle Bizi Sunday wore his working clothes. Only Anna Hibiscus looked pretty and smart. Grandmother sighed when she saw her. But she didn't say why.

Down by the lagoon there were many, many people all pushing and squeezing and rushing to get on and off the ferry. Anna Hibiscus held tight to Uncle Bizi Sunday's hand. A man with strong legs was keeping the ferry in place. He had one foot on the jetty and one foot in the ferry. Auntie Joly jumped onto the ferry. Uncle Bizi Sunday jumped onto the ferry. Anna Hibiscus had to jump too. She had to jump if she wanted to go to the other side of the city.

Uncle Bizi Sunday held out his arms to Anna Hibiscus. As Anna jumped, a big woman jumped too, bumping Anna and rocking the ferry. Anna almost fell into the lagoon, but Uncle Bizi Sunday caught her arm quick-quick and pulled her into the boat. One of Anna Hibiscus's pink flip-flops fell into the lagoon. It floated away with the rest of the rubbish under the boat and was gone.

"Do you want to kill my brother's child?"
Auntie Joly shouted. "Wha' kind of woman
are you? Ca' you not see a child when she
is jumping in front of you?"

Quickly the woman said, "Sorry, ma. Sorry."
She looked at Anna Hibiscus. "Don' cry.
Don' cry," she said.

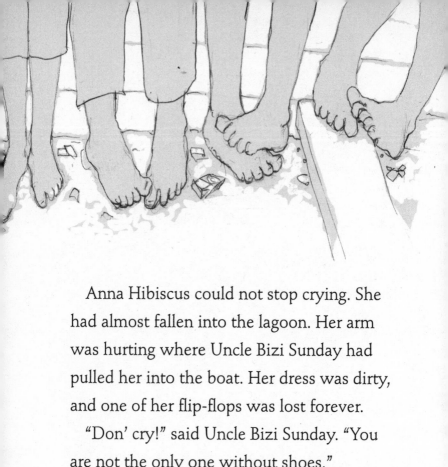

Anna Hibiscus could not stop crying. She
had almost fallen into the lagoon. Her arm
was hurting where Uncle Bizi Sunday had
pulled her into the boat. Her dress was dirty,
and one of her flip-flops was lost forever.

"Don' cry!" said Uncle Bizi Sunday. "You
are not the only one without shoes."

Anna Hibiscus looked. Most of the people
on the ferry had no shoes. Their bare feet

rested in the rubbish and the dirty water
in the bottom of the boat. Just like Anna's
one bare foot.

Anna stopped crying. She kept on her
other flip-flop. What else could she do? Anna
Hibiscus worried. Would people on the other
side of the city notice her beautiful dress
and her pretty ribbons and her shiny hair,
or would they only notice her one shoe?

The overloaded ferry reached the other
side of the lagoon, and Uncle Bizi Sunday
carried Anna Hibiscus down from the boat.
Anna looked around.

The first person she saw was a beggar
girl holding her hands out for coins. Her
hair was ragged and matted into dusty,
dirty clumps. She had no legs.

The beggar girl looked at Anna Hibiscus
and called out, "Fine girl, help me. Fine girl,
help your sister!"

Anna Hibiscus did not know what to do.
She did not want to look at the beggar girl
with no legs. She had no money to help
this new "sister" who was like no other girl
she had seen before, rich or poor. So Anna
hid behind Auntie
Joly until they had
moved away.

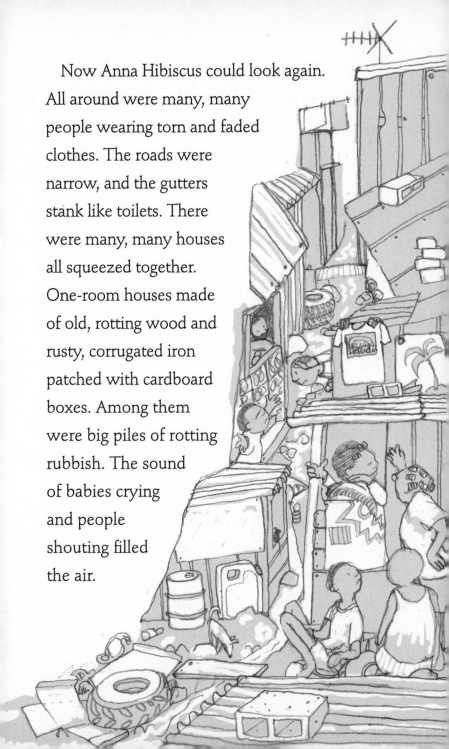

Now Anna Hibiscus could look again.
All around were many, many
people wearing torn and faded
clothes. The roads were
narrow, and the gutters
stank like toilets. There
were many, many houses
all squeezed together.
One-room houses made
of old, rotting wood and
rusty, corrugated iron
patched with cardboard
boxes. Among them
were big piles of rotting
rubbish. The sound
of babies crying
and people
shouting filled
the air.

Anna Hibiscus had never seen anything like this before. She wanted to close her eyes and close her nose and close her ears and make it all go away, but her eyes and nose and ears stayed open and wide. She held tight to Auntie Joly's hand.

Auntie Joly and Uncle Bizi Sunday stopped outside a one-room house made of corrugated iron full of rusty holes. A weak voice called for them to enter. It was hot inside. The sun beat down on the iron walls and roof, heating the room like an oven. It was too hot for Anna Hibiscus.

"Anna Hibiscus, go and wait for us outside," Auntie Joly said, after she had greeted the sick, old woman lying on a mat.

Outside, it was not so hot. The sun still beat down, but there was air. Close to Anna Hibiscus was a pile of rubbish. A big pile of rubbish. There were children climbing all over it.

Anna went closer. The children were naked or clothed in rags. They were picking things out of the rubbish. They were *eating* the rubbish!

Anna Hibiscus could not blink or even think. Suddenly she no longer knew why she was wearing her best pink Sunday dress and her favorite ribbons. She hoped none of the children would notice, or they would know she did not have to eat rubbish. They would know she had pretty dresses while they ate rubbish.

Anna Hibiscus saw one girl, dressed only in ragged underpants, pick a flip-flop out of the rubbish. It was pink. The same as Anna's. The girl tried it on. It fitted. She was the same size as Anna Hibiscus!

The girl saw Anna Hibiscus watching her. They looked at each other, and the girl frowned. Anna Hibiscus was wearing her best pink dress. She had pretty ribbons in her hair. The girl was wearing ragged gray underpants. Her hair was all cut off. But they were both wearing only one pink flip-flop. Anna Hibiscus smiled at the girl. The girl gave Anna Hibiscus a crooked smile back.

Slowly, Anna Hibiscus took off her one pink flip-flop. She held it out to the girl.

The girl shook her head and frowned.
So Anna Hibiscus put her flip-flop on the
pile of rubbish and turned her back on it.
Quickly, before anyone else could, the girl
picked up the flip-flop and put it on.

Anna Hibiscus looked around and saw the
girl skipping away down the street in her
matching pink flip-flops. Anna gazed at the
other naked, ragged children. She thought of
her many dresses hanging in the cupboard
in her room. And Anna Hibiscus took off her
dress. She took it off right there in the street
and threw it onto
the rubbish heap.

When Auntie Joly and
Uncle Bizi Sunday
came out, Anna
Hibiscus was waiting
for them. She looked
almost like the other
children. Except she was
clean and so were her white
pants, and she also had
ribbons in her hair.

"Way-tin happen?"
Uncle Bizi Sunday cried.

"Anna Hibiscus!" shouted Auntie Joly.
"What kind of nonsense is this?"

Anna Hibiscus did not answer. She was
watching a small girl dancing down the road
in a pink Sunday dress. She looked at Auntie
Joly and Uncle Bizi Sunday and smiled her
biggest smile.

Auntie Joly gasped and closed her eyes. Uncle Bizi Sunday shook his head. "Anna Hibiscus!" he said.

"Grandmother will deal with you at home, Anna Hibiscus," Auntie Joly said, and she led her back to the ferry.

The beggar girl was still there by the jetty. She saw Anna Hibiscus. Anna did not look so fine now. But she was feeling better than before. She took her favorite ribbons from her hair and tied them softly, softly in the matted hair of the beggar girl with no legs.

The beggar girl looked at Anna Hibiscus with wide eyes. "God bless you!" she whispered.

And that is exactly what Grandmother said after Anna Hibiscus explained to the gathered family why she had come home in only her underpants.

"Hooray!" said Double.

"Hooray for Anna 'biscus!"
said Trouble.

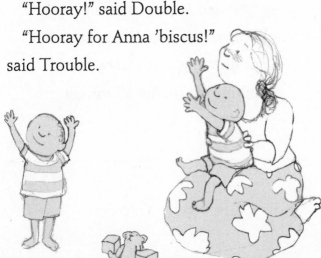

Atinuke was born in Nigeria and spent her childhood in both Africa and the UK. She works as a traditional oral storyteller in schools and theaters all over the world. Atinuke lives on a mountain overlooking the sea in West Wales. She supports the charity SOS Children's Villages.

Lauren Tobia lives in Southville, Bristol. She shares her tiny house with her husband and their two yappy Jack Russell terriers. When Lauren is not drawing, she can be found drinking tea on her allotment.